# Hydroplanes

BY DENNY VON FINN

FORMULA

0-5

5

FORMULA

FORMULA

FORMULA

TORQUE™

BELLWETHER MEDIA • MINNEAPOLIS, MN

**TORQUE**™

Are you ready to take it to the extreme? Torque books thrust you into the action-packed world of sports, vehicles, and adventure. These books may include dirt, smoke, fire, and dangerous stunts.

WARNING: READ AT YOUR OWN RISK.

This edition first published in 2009 by Bellwether Media.

No part of this publication may be reproduced in whole or in part without written permission of the publisher. For information regarding permission, write to Bellwether Media Inc., Attention: Permissions Department, Post Office Box 19349, Minneapolis, MN 55419.

Library of Congress Cataloging-in-Publication Data
Von Finn, Denny.
 Hydroplanes / by Denny Von Finn.
    p. cm. — (Torque. Cool rides)
 Includes bibliographical references and index.
 Summary: "Amazing photography accompanies engaging information about Hydroplanes. The combination of high-interest subject matter and light text is intended for readers in grades 3 through 7"—Provided by publisher.
  ISBN-13: 978-1-60014-211-6 (hardcover : alk. paper)
  ISBN-10: 1-60014-211-7 (hardcover : alk. paper)
  1. Hydroplanes—Juvenile literature. I. Title.

VM341.V66 2009
623.82'314—dc22                          2008017018

# Contents

# What Is a Hydroplane?

A hydroplane is a motorboat built for racing. Drivers compete on rivers and lakes. Today's hydroplanes can reach speeds of more than 200 miles (322 kilometers) per hour.

The word "hydroplane" is made up of two words. *Hydro* means "water." *Plane* means to skim across a surface. A hydroplane barely touches the water's surface. This helps a hydroplane reach great speeds. This can also make a hydroplane difficult to control, sometimes resulting in crashes.

## Fast FaCt

Australian Ken Warby set the world's water speed record in a jet-powered hydroplane. On October 8, 1978, he drove *Miss Australia* to a speed of 317.596 miles (511.11 kilometers) per hour!

# Hydroplane History

Hydroplanes were first made in the early 1900s. Boat-builder Christopher Columbus Smith is credited with developing the hydroplane. Early hydroplanes were made of wood. They were powered by aircraft engines.

Hydroplanes changed a lot after World War II. Boat-builders began to use lighter materials such as **fiberglass**. Lighter materials made the boats even faster.

EMPIRE DAY

## Fast FaCt

The Gold Cup is the oldest prize in boat racing. It was first awarded in 1904. It has been won by a hydroplane every year since 1911.

Hydroplanes come in many sizes. The smallest have 10-**horsepower** engines. **Unlimited Light** boats are large hydroplanes. These boats are powered by automobile engines. **Unlimited** hydroplanes are the largest, most powerful, and most popular kind of hydroplane. Some Unlimited hydroplanes are powered by helicopter engines!

# Parts of a Hydroplane

Hydroplanes look different from other boats. One large **sponson** is located on each side of the **bow** to help the hydroplane balance. An Unlimited hydroplane **cockpit** has a cover called a canopy that protects the driver in a crash.

Unlimited hydroplanes have **turbine** helicopter engines. They can produce 2,650 horsepower! That's more than 12 times the power of a normal car engine. The fastest speed ever recorded by an Unlimited hydroplane is 318.75 miles (510 kilometers) per hour.

All hydroplane engines turn a **propeller** at the rear of the boat. The spinning propeller pushes the boat across the water. Only the sponsons and propeller touch the water during a race. This means there is little **friction** between the boat and the water. Friction slows an object moving across a surface.

Reduced friction also means a hydroplane can easily flip over. A **wing** is located at the rear of the hydroplane. Air that passes over the wing pushes downward on the boat. This helps keep the hydroplane from tipping over.

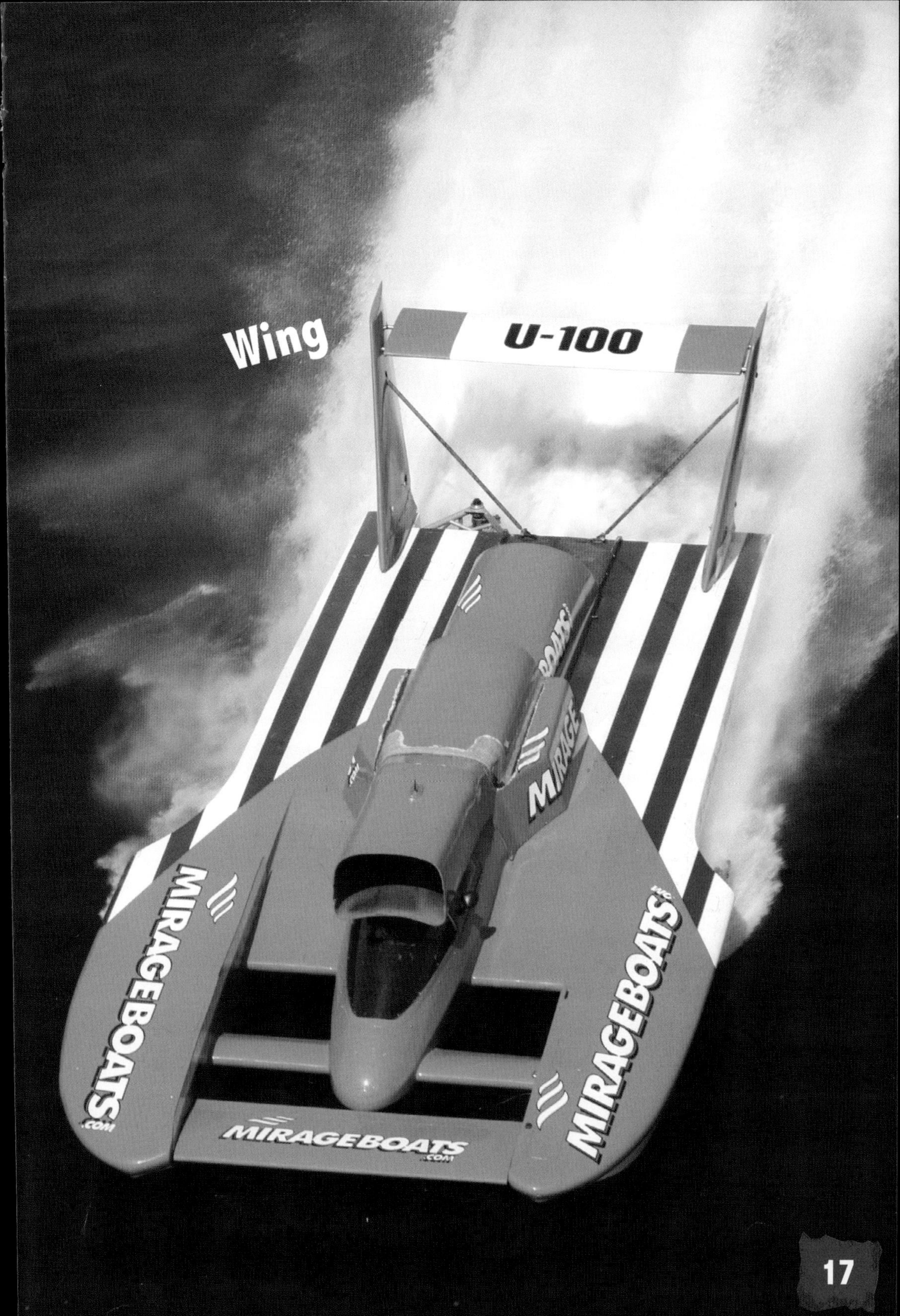

Wing

U-100

MIRAGEBOATS.com

MIRAGE

MIRAGEBOATS.com

MIRAGEBOATS.com

17

# HyDroplanes in Action

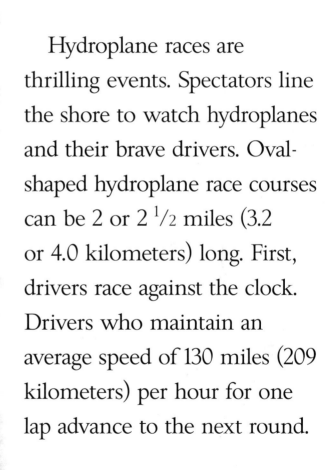

Hydroplane races are thrilling events. Spectators line the shore to watch hydroplanes and their brave drivers. Oval-shaped hydroplane race courses can be 2 or 2 $\frac{1}{2}$ miles (3.2 or 4.0 kilometers) long. First, drivers race against the clock. Drivers who maintain an average speed of 130 miles (209 kilometers) per hour for one lap advance to the next round.

Up to six boats compete against each other in the next round. The drivers fight for position. They use foot pedals to steer the boat around the **buoys**.

The most successful drivers will race in
the final the next day. The winner of the
final is crowned champion of the event.

# Glossary

**bow**—the front of a hydroplane

**buoys**—floating objects placed in the water to mark a hydroplane course

**cockpit**—the area of the hydroplane where the driver sits

**fiberglass**—a hard material used to make modern boats

**friction**—a resistance to movement created when two surfaces rub against each other

**horsepower**—a unit for measuring the power of an engine

**propeller**—a spinning, three-bladed device at the back of the hydroplane that pushes it forward

**sponson**—a large, cylinder-shaped extension on each side of the bow that creates a tunnel of air beneath the hydroplane

**turbine**—an engine that has turning blades that create power

**Unlimited**—the most powerful class of competition hydroplanes

**Unlimited Light**—a class of hydroplanes powered by automotive engines

**wing**—a high, flat surface attached to the back of a hydroplane to help keep it from flipping over

# To Learn mOre

## AT THE LIBRARY

Bornhoft, Simon. *High-Speed Boats: The Need for Speed*. Minneapolis, Minn.: Lerner, 1999.

Savage, Jeff. *Hydroplane Boats*. Mankato, Minn.: Capstone, 2004.

Strobel Dieker, Wendy. *Hydroplanes*. Mankato, Minn.: Capstone, 2007.

## ON THE WEB

Learning more about hydroplanes

is as easy as 1, 2, 3.

1. Go to www.factsurfer.com

2. Enter "hydroplanes" into search box.

3. Click the "Surf" button and you will
   see a list of related web sites.

With factsurfer.com, finding more information is just a click away.

# Index